THE THANKSGIVING VISITOR

A CHRISTMAS MEMORY

THE

THANKSGIVING

VISITOR

Truman

RANDOM HOUSE

A CHRISTMAS

MEMORY

Capote

NEW YORK

THE THANKSGIVING VISITOR

for Lee

Talk about mean! Odd Henderson was the meanest human creature in my experience.

And I'm speaking of a twelve-year-old boy, not some grownup who has had the time to ripen a naturally evil disposition. At least, Odd was twelve in 1932, when we were both second-graders attending a small-town school in rural Alabama.

Tall for his age, a bony boy with muddy-red hair and

narrow yellow eyes, he towered over all his classmates—
would have in any event, for the rest of us were only seven
or eight years old. Odd had failed first grade twice and
was now serving his second term in the second grade.
This sorry record wasn't due to dumbness—Odd was
intelligent, maybe cunning is a better word—but he took
after the rest of the Hendersons. The whole family (there
were ten of them, not counting Dad Henderson, who was
a bootlegger and usually in jail, all scrunched together in
a four-room house next door to a Negro church) was a
shiftless, surly bunch, every one of them ready to do you
a bad turn; Odd wasn't the worst of the lot, and brother,
that is *saying* something.

Many children in our school came from families poorer
than the Hendersons; Odd had a pair of shoes, while some
boys, girls too, were forced to go barefoot right through
the bitterest weather—that's how hard the Depression
had hit Alabama. But nobody, I don't care who, looked as

down-and-out as Odd—a skinny, freckled scarecrow in sweaty cast-off overalls that would have been a humiliation to a chain-gang convict. You might have felt pity for him if he hadn't been so hateful. All the kids feared him, not just us younger kids, but even boys his own age and older.

Nobody ever picked a fight with him except one time a girl named Ann "Jumbo" Finchburg, who happened to be the other town bully. Jumbo, a sawed-off but solid tomboy with an all-hell-let-loose wrestling technique, jumped Odd from behind during recess one dull morning, and it took three teachers, each of whom must have wished the combatants would kill each other, a good long while to separate them. The result was a sort of draw: Jumbo lost a tooth and half her hair and developed a grayish cloud in her left eye (she never could see clear again); Odd's afflictions included a broken thumb, plus scratch scars that will stay with him to the day they shut his coffin. For months afterward, Odd played every kind of trick to goad Jumbo

11

into a rematch; but Jumbo had gotten her licks and gave him considerable berth. As I would have done if he'd let me; alas, I was the object of Odd's relentless attentions.

Considering the era and locale, I was fairly well off—living, as I did, in a high-ceilinged old country house situated where the town ended and the farms and forests began. The house belonged to distant relatives, elderly cousins, and these cousins, three maiden ladies and their bachelor brother, had taken me under their roof because of a disturbance among my more immediate family, a custody battle that, for involved reasons, had left me stranded in this somewhat eccentric Alabama household. Not that I was unhappy there; indeed, moments of those few years turned out to be the happiest part of an otherwise difficult childhood, mainly because the youngest of the cousins, a woman in her sixties, became my first friend. As she was a child herself (many people thought her less than that, and murmured about her as though she were the twin of poor nice Lester Tucker, who roamed the streets in a sweet daze), she understood children, and understood me absolutely.

Perhaps it was strange for a young boy to have as his best friend an aging spinster, but neither of us had an ordinary outlook or background, and so it was inevitable, in our separate loneliness, that we should come to share a friendship apart. Except for the hours I spent at school, the three of us, me and old Queenie, our feisty little rat terrier, and Miss Sook, as everyone called my friend, were almost always together. We hunted herbs in the woods, went fishing on remote creeks (with dried sugarcane stalks for fishing poles) and gathered curious ferns and greeneries that we transplanted and grew with trailing flourish in tin pails and chamber pots. Mostly, though, our life was lived in the kitchen—a farmhouse kitchen, dominated by a big black wood-burning stove, that was often dark and sunny at the same time.

Miss Sook, sensitive as shy-lady fern, a recluse who had never traveled beyond the county boundaries, was totally unlike her brother and sisters, the latter being down-to-earth, vaguely masculine ladies who operated a dry-goods store and several other business ventures. The brother, Uncle B., owned a number of cotton farms scattered around the countryside; because he refused to drive a car or endure any contact whatever with mobilized machinery, he rode horseback, jogging all day from one property to another. He was a kind man, though a silent one: he grunted yes or no, and really never opened his mouth except to feed it. At every meal he had the appetite of an Alaskan grizzly after a winter's hibernation, and it was Miss Sook's task to fill him up.

Breakfast was our principal meal; midday dinner, except on Sundays, and supper were casual menus, often composed of leftovers from the morning. These breakfasts, served promptly at 5:30 A.M., were regular stomach

14

swellers. To the present day I retain a nostalgic hunger for those cockcrow repasts of ham and fried chicken, fried pork chops, fried catfish, fried squirrel (in season), fried eggs, hominy grits with gravy, black-eyed peas, collards with collard liquor and cornbread to mush it in, biscuits, pound cake, pancakes and molasses, honey in the comb, homemade jams and jellies, sweet milk, buttermilk, coffee chicory-flavored and hot as Hades.

The cook, accompanied by her assistants, Queenie and myself, rose every morning at four to fire the stove and set the table and get everything started. Rising at that hour was not the hardship it may sound; we were used to it, and anyway we always went to bed as soon as the sun dropped and the birds had settled in the trees. Also, my friend was not as frail as she seemed; though she had been sickly as a child and her shoulders were hunched, she had strong hands and sturdy legs. She could move with sprightly, purposeful speed, the frayed tennis shoes she invariably wore squeaking on the waxed kitchen floor, and her distinguished face, with its delicately clumsy features and beautiful, youthful eyes, bespoke a fortitude that suggested it was more the reward of an interior spiritual shine than the visible surface of mere mortal health.

Nevertheless, depending on the season and the number of hands employed on Uncle B.'s farms, there were sometimes as many as fifteen people sitting down to those dawn banquets; the hands were entitled to one hot meal a day—it was part of their wages. Supposedly, a Negro woman came in to help wash the dishes, make the beds, clean the house and do the laundry. She was lazy and unreliable but a lifelong friend of Miss Sook's—which meant that my friend would not consider replacing her and simply did the work herself. She chopped firewood, tended a large menagerie of chickens, turkeys and hogs, scrubbed, dusted, mended all our clothes; yet when I came home from school, she was always eager to keep me company—to play a card game named Rook or rush off on a mushroom hunt or have a pillow fight or, as we sat in the kitchen's waning afternoon light, help me with homework.

She loved to pore over my textbooks, the geography atlas especially ("Oh, Buddy," she would say, because she called me Buddy, "just think of it—a lake named Titicaca. That really exists somewhere in the world"). My education was her education, as well. Due to her childhood illness, she had had almost no schooling; her handwriting was a series of jagged eruptions, the spelling a highly personal and phonetic affair. I could already write and read with a smoother assurance than she was capable of (though she managed to "study" one Bible chapter every day, and never missed "Little Orphan Annie" or "The Katzenjammer Kids," comics carried by the Mobile paper). She took a bristling pride in "our" report cards ("Gosh, Buddy! Five A's. Even arithmetic. I didn't dare to hope we'd get an A in arithmetic"). It was a mystery to her why I hated school, why some mornings I wept and pleaded with Uncle B., the deciding voice in the house, to let me stay home.

Of course it wasn't that I hated school; what I hated was Odd Henderson. The torments he contrived! For instance, he used to wait for me in the shadows under a water oak that darkened an edge of the school grounds; in his hand he held a paper sack stuffed with prickly cockleburs collected on his way to school. There was no sense in trying to outrun him, for he was quick as a coiled snake; like a rattler, he struck, slammed me to the ground and, his slitty eyes gleeful, rubbed the burrs into my scalp. Usually a circle of kids ganged around to titter, or pretend to; they didn't really think it funny; but Odd made them nervous and ready to please. Later, hiding in a toilet in the boys' room, I would untangle the burrs knotting my hair; this took forever and always meant missing the first bell.

Our second-grade teacher, Miss Armstrong, was sympathetic, for she suspected what was happening; but eventually, exasperated by my continual tardiness, she raged at me in front of the whole class: "Little mister big britches. What a big head he has! Waltzing in here twenty minutes after the bell. A half hour." Whereupon I lost control; I pointed at Odd Henderson and shouted: "Yell at him. He's the one to blame. The sonafabitch."

I knew a lot of curse words, yet even I was shocked when I heard what I'd said resounding in an awful silence, and Miss Armstrong, advancing toward me clutching a heavy ruler, said, "Hold out your hands, sir. Palms up, sir." Then, while Odd Henderson watched with a small citric smile, she blistered the palms of my hands with her brass-edged ruler until the room blurred.

It would take a page in small print to list the imaginative punishments Odd inflicted, but what I resented and suffered from most was the sense of dour expectations he induced. Once, when he had me pinned against a wall, I asked him straight out what had I done to make him dislike me so much; suddenly he relaxed, let me loose and said, "You're a sissy. I'm just straightening you out." He was right, I was a sissy of sorts, and the moment he said it, I realized there was nothing I could do to alter his judgment, other than toughen myself to accept and defend the fact.

As soon as I regained the peace of the warm kitchen, where Queenie might be gnawing an old dug-up bone and my friend puttering with a piecrust, the weight of Odd Henderson would blessedly slide from my shoulders. But too often at night, the narrow lion eyes loomed in my dreams while his high, harsh voice, pronouncing cruel promises, hissed in my ears.

My friend's bedroom was next to mine; occasionally cries arising from my nightmare upheavals wakened her; then she would come and shake me out of an Odd Henderson coma. "Look," she'd say, lighting a lamp, "you've even scared Queenie. She's shaking." And, "Is it a fever?

You're wringing wet. Maybe we ought to call Doctor Stone." But she knew that it wasn't a fever, she knew that it was because of my troubles at school, for I had told and told her how Odd Henderson treated me.

But now I'd stopped talking about it, never mentioned it any more, because she refused to acknowledge that any human could be as bad as I made him out. Innocence, preserved by the absence of experience that had always isolated Miss Sook, left her incapable of encompassing an evil so complete.

"Oh," she might say, rubbing heat into my chilled hands, "he only picks on you out of jealousy. He's not smart and pretty as you are." Or, less jestingly, "The thing to keep in mind, Buddy, is this boy can't help acting ugly; he doesn't know any different. All those Henderson children have had it hard. And you can lay that at Dad Henderson's door. I don't like to say it, but that man never was anything except a mischief and a fool. Did you know Uncle B. horsewhipped him once? Caught him beating a dog and horsewhipped him on the spot. The best thing that ever happened was when they locked him up at State Farm. But I remember Molly Henderson before she married Dad. Just fifteen or sixteen she was, and fresh from somewhere across the river. She worked for Sade Danvers down the road, learning to be a dressmaker. She used to pass here and see me hoeing in the garden— such a polite girl, with lovely red hair, and so appreciative of everything; sometimes I'd give her a bunch of sweet peas or a japonica, and she was always so appreciative. Then she began strolling by arm in arm with Dad Henderson—and him so much older and a perfect rascal, drunk or sober. Well, the Lord must have His reasons. But it's a shame; Molly can't be more than thirty-five, and there she is without a tooth in her head or a dime to her name. Nothing but a houseful of children to feed. You've got to take all that into account, Buddy, and be patient."

Patient! What was the use of discussing it? Finally, though, my friend did comprehend the seriousness of my despair. The realization arrived in a quiet way and was not the outcome of unhappy midnight wakings or pleading scenes with Uncle B. It happened one rainy November twilight when we were sitting alone in the kitchen close by the dying stove fire; supper was over, the dishes stacked, and Queenie was tucked in a rocker, snoring. I could hear my friend's whispery voice weaving under the skipping noise of rain on the roof, but my mind was on my worries and I was not attending, though I was aware that her subject was Thanksgiving, then a week away.

My cousins had never married (Uncle B. had *almost* married, but his fiancée returned the engagement ring when she saw that sharing a house with three very individual spinsters would be part of the bargain); however, they boasted extensive family connections throughout the vicinity: cousins aplenty, and an aunt, Mrs. Mary Taylor

Wheelwright, who was one hundred and three years old. As our house was the largest and the most conveniently located, it was traditional for these relations to aim themselves our way every year at Thanksgiving; though there were seldom fewer than thirty celebrants, it was not an onerous chore, because we provided only the setting and an ample number of stuffed turkeys.

The guests supplied the trimmings, each of them contributing her particular specialty: a cousin twice removed, Harriet Parker from Flomaton, made perfect ambrosia, transparent orange slices combined with freshly ground coconut; Harriet's sister Alice usually arrived carrying a dish of whipped sweet potatoes and raisins; the Conklin tribe, Mr. and Mrs. Bill Conklin and their quartet of handsome daughters, always brought a delicious array of vegetables canned during the summer. My own favorite was a cold banana pudding—a guarded recipe of the ancient aunt who, despite her longevity, was still domestically energetic; to our sorrow she took the secret with her when she died in 1934, age one hundred and five (and it wasn't age that lowered the curtain; she was attacked and trampled by a bull in a pasture).

Miss Sook was ruminating on these matters while my mind wandered through a maze as melancholy as the wet twilight. Suddenly I heard her knuckles rap the kitchen table: "Buddy!"

"What?"

"You haven't listened to one word."

"Sorry."

"I figure we'll need five turkeys this year. When I spoke to Uncle B. about it, he said he wanted you to kill them. Dress them, too."

"But *why?*"

"He says a boy ought to know how to do things like that."

Slaughtering was Uncle B.'s job. It was an ordeal for

me to watch him butcher a hog or even wring a chicken's neck. My friend felt the same way; neither of us could abide any violence bloodier than swatting flies, so I was taken aback at her casual relaying of this command.

"Well, I won't."

Now she smiled. "Of course you won't. I'll get Bubber or some other colored boy. Pay him a nickel. But," she said, her tone descending conspiratorially, "we'll let Uncle B. believe it was you. Then he'll be pleased and stop saying it's such a bad thing."

"What's a bad thing?"

"Our always being together. He says you ought to have other friends, boys your own age. Well, he's right."

"I don't want any other friend."

"Hush, Buddy. Now hush. You've been real good to me. I don't know what I'd do without you. Just become an old crab. But I want to see you happy, Buddy. Strong, able to go out in the world. And you're never going to until you come to terms with people like Odd Henderson and turn them into friends."

"Him! He's the last friend in the world I want."

"Please, Buddy—invite that boy here for Thanksgiving dinner."

Though the pair of us occasionally quibbled, we never quarreled. At first I was unable to believe she meant her request as something more than a sample of poor-taste humor; but then, seeing that she was serious, I realized, with bewilderment, that we were edging toward a falling-out.

"I thought you were my *friend*."

"I am, Buddy. Truly."

"If you were, you couldn't think up a thing like that. Odd Henderson hates me. He's my *enemy*."

"He can't hate you. He doesn't know you."

"Well, I hate him."

"Because you don't know him. That's all I ask. The chance for you to know each other a little. Then I think this trouble will stop. And maybe you're right, Buddy, maybe you boys won't ever be friends. But I doubt that he'd pick on you any more."

"You don't understand. You've never hated anybody."

"No, I never have. We're allotted just so much time on earth, and I wouldn't want the Lord to see me wasting mine in any such manner."

"I won't do it. He'd think I was crazy. And I would be."

The rain had let up, leaving a silence that lengthened miserably. My friend's clear eyes contemplated me as though I were a Rook card she was deciding how to play; she maneuvered a salt-pepper lock of hair off her forehead and sighed. "Then *I* will. Tomorrow," she said, "I'll put on my hat and pay a call on Molly Henderson." This statement certified her determination, for I'd never known Miss Sook to plan a call on anyone, not only because she was entirely without social talent, but also because she was too modest to presume a welcome. "I don't suppose there will be much Thanksgiving in their house. Probably Molly would be very pleased to have Odd sit down with us. Oh, I know Uncle B. would never permit it, but the nice thing to do is invite them all."

My laughter woke Queenie; and after a surprised instant, my friend laughed too. Her cheeks pinked and a light flared in her eyes; rising, she hugged me and said, "Oh, Buddy, I knew you'd forgive me and recognize there was some sense to my notion."

She was mistaken. My merriment had other origins. Two. One was the picture of Uncle B. carving turkey for all those cantankerous Hendersons. The second was: It had occurred to me that I had no cause for alarm; Miss Sook might extend the invitation and Odd's mother might accept it in his behalf; but Odd wouldn't show up in a million years.

He would be too proud. For instance, throughout the Depression years, our school distributed free milk and sandwiches to all children whose families were too poor to provide them with a lunch box. But Odd, emaciated as he was, refused to have anything to do with these hand-outs; he'd wander off by himself and devour a pocketful of peanuts or gnaw a large raw turnip. This kind of pride was characteristic of the Henderson breed: they might steal, gouge the gold out of a dead man's teeth, but they would never accept a gift offered openly, for anything smacking of charity was offensive to them. Odd was sure to figure Miss Sook's invitation as a charitable gesture; or see it—and not incorrectly—as a blackmailing stunt meant to make him ease up on me.

I went to bed that night with a light heart, for I was certain my Thanksgiving would not be marred by the presence of such an unsuitable visitor.

The next morning I had a bad cold, which was pleasant; it meant no school. It also meant I could have a fire in my room and cream-of-tomato soup and hours alone with

Mr. Micawber and David Copperfield: the happiest of stayabeds. It was drizzling again; but true to her promise, my friend fetched her hat, a straw cartwheel decorated with weather-faded velvet roses, and set out for the Henderson home. "I won't be but a minute," she said. In fact, she was gone the better part of two hours. I couldn't imagine Miss Sook sustaining so long a conversation except with me or herself (she talked to herself often, a habit of sane persons of a solitary nature); and when she returned, she did seem drained.

Still wearing her hat and an old loose raincoat, she slipped a thermometer in my mouth, then sat at the foot of the bed. "I like her," she said firmly. "I always have liked Molly Henderson. She does all she can, and the house was clean as Bob Spencer's fingernails"— Bob Spencer being a Baptist minister famed for his hygienic gleam—"but bitter cold. With a tin roof and the wind right in the room and not a scrap of fire in the fireplace.

She offered me refreshment, and I surely would have welcomed a cup of coffee, but I said no. Because I don't expect there was any coffee on the premises. Or sugar.

"It made me feel ashamed, Buddy. It hurts me all the way down to see somebody struggling like Molly. Never able to see a clear day. I don't say people should have everything they want. Though, come to think of it, I don't see what's wrong with that, either. You ought to have a bike to ride, and why shouldn't Queenie have a beef bone every day? Yes, now it's come to me, now I understand: We really all of us ought to have everything we want. I'll bet you a dime that's what the Lord intends. And when all around us we see people who can't satisfy the plainest needs, I feel ashamed. Oh, not of myself, because who am I, an old nobody who never owned a mite; if I hadn't had a family to pay my way, I'd have starved or been sent to the County Home. The shame I feel is for all of us who have anything extra when other people have nothing.

"I mentioned to Molly how we had more quilts here than we could ever use—there's a trunk of scrap quilts in the attic, the ones I made when I was a girl and couldn't go outdoors much. But she cut me off, said the Hendersons were doing just fine, thank you, and the only thing they wanted was Dad to be set free and sent home to his people. 'Miss Sook,' she told me, 'Dad is a good husband, no matter what else he might be.' Meanwhile, she has her children to care for.

"And, Buddy, you must be wrong about her boy Odd. At least partially. Molly says he's a great help to her and a great comfort. Never complains, regardless of how many chores she gives him. Says he can sing good as you hear on the radio, and when the younger children start raising a ruckus, he can quiet them down by singing to them. Bless us," she lamented, retrieving the thermometer, "all we can do for people like Molly is respect them and remember them in our prayers."

The thermometer had kept me silent; now I demanded, "But what about the invitation?"

"Sometimes," she said, scowling at the scarlet thread in the glass, "I think these eyes are giving out. At my age, a body starts to look around very closely. So you'll remember how cobwebs really looked. But to answer your question, Molly was happy to hear you thought enough of Odd to ask him over for Thanksgiving. And," she continued, ignoring my groan, "she said she was sure he'd be tickled to come. Your temperature is just over the hundred mark. I guess you can count on staying home tomorrow. That ought to bring smiles! Let's see you smile, Buddy."

As it happened, I was smiling a good deal during the next few days prior to the big feast, for my cold had advanced to croup and I was out of school the entire period. I had no contact with Odd Henderson and therefore could not personally ascertain his reaction to the invitation; but I imagined it must have made him laugh first and spit next. The prospect of his actually appearing didn't worry me; it was as farfetched a possibility as Queenie snarling at me or Miss Sook betraying my trust in her.

Yet Odd remained a presence, a redheaded silhouette on the threshold of my cheerfulness. Still, I was tantalized by the description his mother had provided; I wondered if it was true he had another side, that somewhere underneath the evil a speck of humaneness existed. But that was impossible! Anybody who believed so would leave their house unlocked when the gypsies came to town. All you had to do was look at him.

Miss Sook was aware that my croup was not as severe as I pretended, and so in the mornings, when the others had absented themselves—Uncle B. to his farms and the sisters to their dry-goods store—she tolerated my getting out of bed and even let me assist in the springlike housecleaning that always preceded the Thanksgiving assembly.

There was such a lot to do, enough for a dozen hands. We polished the parlor furniture, the piano, the black curio cabinet (which contained only a fragment of Stone Mountain the sisters had brought back from a business trip to Atlanta), the formal walnut rockers and florid Biedermeier pieces—rubbed them with lemon-scented wax until the place was shiny as lemon skin and smelled like a citrus grove. Curtains were laundered and rehung, pillows punched, rugs beaten; wherever one glanced, dust motes and tiny feathers drifted in the sparkling November light sifting through the tall rooms. Poor Queenie was relegated to the kitchen, for fear she might leave a stray hair, perhaps a flea, in the more dignified areas of the house.

The most delicate task was preparing the napkins and tablecloths that would decorate the dining room. The linen had belonged to my friend's mother, who had received it as a wedding gift; though it had been used only once or twice a year, say two hundred times in the past eighty years, nevertheless it was eighty years old, and mended patches and freckled discolorations were apparent. Probably it had not been a fine material to begin with, but Miss Sook treated it as though it had been woven by golden hands on heavenly looms: "My mother said, 'The day may come when all we can offer is well water and cold cornbread, but at least we'll be able to serve it on a table set with proper linen.' "

At night, after the day's dashing about and when the rest of the house was dark, one feeble lamp burned late while my friend, propped in bed with napkins massed on her lap, repaired blemishes and tears with thread and needle, her forehead crumpled, her eyes cruelly squeezed, yet illuminated by the fatigued rapture of a pilgrim approaching an altar at journey's end.

From hour to hour, as the shivery tolls of the faraway courthouse clock numbered ten and eleven and twelve, I would wake up and see her lamp still lit, and would drowsily lurch into her room to reprimand her: "You ought to be asleep!"

"In a minute, Buddy. I can't just now. When I think of all the company coming, it scares me. Starts my head whirling," she said, ceasing to stitch and rubbing her eyes. "Whirling with stars."

Chrysanthemums: some as big as a baby's head. Bundles of curled penny-colored leaves with flickering lavender underhues. "Chrysanthemums," my friend commented as we moved through our garden stalking flower-show blossoms with decapitating shears, "are like lions. Kingly characters. I always expect them to *spring*. To turn on me with a growl and a roar."

It was the kind of remark that caused people to wonder about Miss Sook, though I understand that only in retrospect, for I always knew just what she meant, and in this instance the whole idea of it, the notion of lugging all those growling gorgeous roaring lions into the house and caging them in tacky vases (our final decorative act on Thanksgiving Eve) made us so giggly and giddy and stupid we were soon out of breath.

"Look at Queenie," my friend said, stuttering with mirth. "Look at her ears, Buddy. Standing straight up. She's thinking, Well, what kind of lunatics are these I'm mixed up with? Ah, Queenie. Come here, honey. I'm going to give you a biscuit dipped in hot coffee."

A lively day, that Thanksgiving. Lively with on-and-off showers and abrupt sky clearings accompanied by thrusts of raw sun and sudden bandit winds snatching autumn's leftover leaves.

The noises of the house were lovely, too: pots and pans and Uncle B.'s unused and rusty voice as he stood in the hall in his creaking Sunday suit, greeting our guests as they arrived. A few came by horseback or mule-drawn wagon, the majority in shined-up farm trucks and rackety flivvers. Mr. and Mrs. Conklin and their four beautiful daughters drove up in a mint-green 1932 Chevrolet (Mr. Conklin was well off; he owned several fishing smackers that operated out of Mobile), an object which aroused warm curiosity among the men present; they studied and poked it and all but took it apart.

The first guests to arrive were Mrs. Mary Taylor Wheelwright, escorted by her custodians, a grandson and his wife. She was a pretty little thing, Mrs. Wheelwright; she wore her age as lightly as the tiny red bonnet that, like the cherry on a vanilla sundae, sat perkily atop her milky hair. "Darlin' Bobby," she said, hugging Uncle B., "I realize we're an itty-bit early, but you know me, always punctual to a fault." Which was an apology deserved, for it was not yet nine o'clock and guests weren't expected much before noon.

However, *everybody* arrived earlier than we intended—except the Perk McCloud family, who suffered two blow-outs in the space of thirty miles and arrived in such a stomping temper, particularly Mr. McCloud, that we feared for the china. Most of these people lived year-round in lonesome places hard to get away from: isolated farms, whistle-stops and crossroads, empty river hamlets or lumber-camp communities deep in the pine forests; so of course it was eagerness that caused them to be early, primed for an affectionate and memorable gathering.

And so it was. Some while ago, I had a letter from one of the Conklin sisters, now the wife of a naval captain and living in San Diego; she wrote: "I think of you often around this time of year, I suppose because of what happened at one of our Alabama Thanksgivings. It was a few years before Miss Sook died—would it be 1933? Golly, I'll never forget that day."

By noon, not another soul could be accommodated in the parlor, a hive humming with women's tattle and womanly aromas: Mrs. Wheelwright smelled of lilac water and Annabel Conklin like geraniums after rain. The odor of tobacco fanned out across the porch, where most of the men had clustered, despite the wavering weather, the alternations between sprinkles of rain and sunlit wind squalls. Tobacco was a substance alien to the setting; true, Miss Sook now and again secretly dipped snuff, a taste acquired under unknown tutelage and one she refused to discuss; her sisters would have been mortified had they suspected, and Uncle B., too, for he took a harsh stand on all stimulants, condemning them morally and medically.

The virile redolence of cigars, the pungent nip of pipe smoke, the tortoiseshell richness they evoked, constantly lured me out of the parlor onto the porch, though it was the parlor I preferred, due to the presence of the Conklin sisters, who played by turn our untuned piano with a gifted, rollicking lack of airs. "Indian Love Call" was among their repertoire, and also a 1918 war ballad, the lament of a child pleading with a house thief, entitled

"Don't Steal Daddy's Medals, He Won Them for Bravery." Annabel played and sang it; she was the oldest of the sisters and the loveliest, though it was a chore to pick among them, for they were like quadruplets of unequal height. One thought of apples, compact and flavorful, sweet but cider-tart; their hair, loosely plaited, had the blue luster of a well-groomed ebony racehorse, and certain features, eyebrows, noses, lips when smiling, tilted in an original style that added humor to their charms. The nicest thing was that they were a bit plump: "pleasingly plump" describes it precisely.

It was while listening to Annabel at the piano, and falling in love with her, that I felt Odd Henderson. I say *felt* because I was aware of him before I saw him: the sense of peril that warns, say, an experienced woodsman of an impending encounter with a rattler or bobcat alerted me.

I turned, and there the fellow stood at the parlor entrance, half in, half out. To others he must have seemed simply a grubby twelve-year-old beanpole who had made some attempt to rise to the event by parting and slicking his difficult hair, the comb grooves were still damply intact. But to me he was as unexpected and sinister as a genie released from a bottle. What a dumbhead I'd been to think he wouldn't show up! Only a dunce wouldn't have guessed that he would come out of spite: the joy of spoiling for me this awaited day.

However, Odd had not yet seen me: Annabel, her firm, acrobatic fingers somersaulting over the warped piano keys, had diverted him, for he was watching her, lips separated, eyes slitted, as though he had come upon her disrobed and cooling herself in the local river. It was as if he were contemplating some wished-for vision; his already red ears had become pimiento. The entrancing scene so dazed him I was able to squeeze directly past him and run along the hall to the kitchen. "He's here!"

My friend had completed her work hours earlier; moreover she had two colored women helping out. Neverthe-less she had been hiding in the kitchen since our party started, under a pretense of keeping the exiled Queenie company. In truth, she was afraid of mingling with any group, even one composed of relatives, which was why, despite her reliance on the Bible and its Hero, she rarely went to church. Although she loved all children and was at ease with them, she was not acceptable as a child, yet she could not accept herself as a peer of grownups and in a collection of them behaved like an awkward young lady, silent and rather astonished. But the *idea* of parties exhil-arated her; what a pity she couldn't take part invisibly, for then how festive she would have felt.

I noticed that my friend's hands were trembling; so were mine. Her usual outfit consisted of calico dresses, tennis shoes and Uncle B.'s discarded sweaters; she had no clothes appropriate to starchy occasions. Today she was lost inside something borrowed from one of her stout sisters, a creepy navy-blue dress its owner had worn to every funeral in the county since time remembered.

"He's here," I informed her for the third time. "Odd Henderson."

"Then why aren't you with him?" she said admonishingly. "That's not polite, Buddy. He's your particular guest. You ought to be out there seeing he meets everybody and has a good time."

"I *can't*. I can't speak to him."

Queenie was curled on her lap, having a head rub; my friend stood up, dumping Queenie and disclosing a stretch of navy-blue material sprinkled with dog hair, said *"Buddy*. You mean you haven't spoken to that boy!" My rudeness obliterated her timidity; taking me by the hand, she steered me to the parlor.

She need not have fretted over Odd's welfare. The charms of Annabel Conklin had drawn him to the piano. Indeed, he was scrunched up beside her on the piano seat,

sitting there studying her delightful profile, his eyes
opaque as the orbs of the stuffed whale I'd seen that summer when a touring honky-tonk passed through town (it
was advertised as *The Original Moby Dick*, and it cost five
cents to view the remains—what a bunch of crooks!). As
for Annabel, she would flirt with anything that walked
or crawled—no, that's unfair, for it was really a form
of generosity, of simply being alive. Still, it gave me
a hurt to see her playing cute with that mule skinner.

Hauling me onward, my friend introduced herself to
him: "Buddy and I, we're so happy you could come." Odd
had the manners of a billy goat: he didn't stand up or
offer his hand, hardly looked at her and at me not at all.
Daunted but dead game, my friend said: "Maybe Odd
will sing us a tune. I know he can; his mother told me so.
Annabel, sugar, play something Odd can sing."

Reading back, I see that I haven't thoroughly described
Odd Henderson's ears—a major omission, for they were

a pair of eye-catchers, like Alfalfa's in the *Our Gang* comedy pictures. Now, because of Annabel's flattering receptivity to my friend's request, his ears became so beet-bright it made your eyes smart. He mumbled, he shook his head hangdog; but Annabel said: "Do you know 'I Have Seen the Light'?" He didn't, but her next suggestion was greeted with a grin of recognition; the biggest fool could tell his modesty was all put on.

Giggling, Annabel struck a rich chord, and Odd, in a voice precociously manly, sang: "When the red, red robin comes bob, bob, bobbin' along." The Adam's apple in his tense throat jumped; Annabel's enthusiasm accelerated; the women's shrill hen chatter slackened as they became aware of the entertainment. Odd was good, he could sing for sure, and the jealousy charging through me had enough power to electrocute a murderer. Murder was what I had in mind; I could have killed him as easily as swat a mosquito. Easier.

Once more, unnoticed even by my friend, who was absorbed in the musicale, I escaped the parlor and sought The Island. That was the name I had given a place in the house where I went when I felt blue or inexplicably exuberant or just when I wanted to think things over. It was a mammoth closet attached to our only bathroom; the bathroom itself, except for its sanitary fixtures, was like a cozy winter parlor, with a horsehair love seat, scatter rugs, a bureau, a fireplace and framed reproductions of "The Doctor's Visit," "September Morn," "The Swan Pool" and calendars galore.

There were two small stained-glass windows in the closet; lozenge-like patterns of rose, amber and green light filtered through the windows, which looked out on the bathroom proper. Here and there patches of color had faded from the glass or been chipped away; by applying an eye to one of these clearings, it was possible to identify the room's visitors. After I'd been secluded there awhile,

brooding over my enemy's success, footsteps intruded:
Mrs. Mary Taylor Wheelwright, who stopped before a
mirror, smacked her face with a powder puff, rouged her
antique cheeks and then, perusing the effect, announced:
"Very nice, Mary. Even if Mary says so herself."

It is well known that women outlive men; could it
merely be superior vanity that keeps them going? Anyway, Mrs. Wheelwright sweetened my mood, so when,
following her departure, a heartily rung dinner bell
sounded through the house, I decided to quit my refuge
and enjoy the feast, regardless of Odd Henderson.

But just then footsteps echoed again. *He* appeared,
looking less sullen than I'd ever seen him. Strutty. Whis-
tling. Unbuttoning his trousers and letting go with a
forceful splash, he whistled along, jaunty as a jaybird in a
field of sunflowers. As he was leaving, an open box on the
bureau summoned his attention. It was a cigar box in
which my friend kept recipes torn out of newspapers and

other junk, as well as a cameo brooch her father had long ago given her. Sentimental value aside, her imagination had conferred upon the object a rare costliness; whenever we had cause for serious grievance against her sisters or Uncle B., she would say, "Never mind, Buddy. We'll sell my cameo and go away. We'll take the bus to New Orleans." Though never discussing what we would do once we arrived in New Orleans, or what we would live on after the cameo money ran out, we both relished this fantasy. Perhaps each of us secretly realized the brooch was only a Sears Roebuck novelty; all the same, it seemed to us a talisman of true, though untested, magic: a charm that promised us our freedom if indeed we did decide to pursue our luck in fabled spheres. So my friend never wore it, for it was too much a treasure to risk its loss or damage.

Now I saw Odd's sacrilegious fingers reach toward it, watched him bounce it in the palm of his hand, drop it back in the box and turn to go. Then return. This time he swiftly retrieved the cameo and sneaked it into his pocket. My boiling first instinct was to rush out of the closet and challenge him; at that moment, I believe I could have pinned Odd to the floor. *But*— Well, do you recall how, in simpler days, funny-paper artists used to illustrate the birth of an idea by sketching an incandescent light bulb above the brow of Mutt or Jeff or whomever? That's how it was with me: a sizzling light bulb suddenly radiated my brain. The shock and brilliance of it made me burn and shiver—laugh, too. Odd had handed me an ideal instrument for revenge, one that would make up for all the cockleburs.

In the dining room, long tables had been joined to shape a T. Uncle B. was at the upper center, Mrs. Mary Taylor Wheelwright at his right and Mrs. Conklin at his left. Odd was seated between two of the Conklin sisters, one of them Annabel, whose compliments kept him in top condition. My friend had put herself at the foot of the table among the youngest children; according to her, she had chosen the position because it provided quicker access to the kitchen, but of course it was because that was where she wished to be. Queenie, who had somehow got loose, was under the table—trembling and wagging with ecstasy as she skittered between the rows of legs—but nobody seemed to object, probably because they were hypnotized by the uncarved, lusciously glazed turkeys and the excellent aromas rising from dishes of okra and corn, onion fritters and hot mince pies.

My own mouth would have watered if it hadn't gone bone-dry at the heart-pounding prospect of total revenge. For a second, glancing at Odd Henderson's suffused face, I experienced a fragmentary regret, but I really had no qualms.

Uncle B. recited grace. Head bowed, eyes shut, calloused hands prayerfully placed, he intoned: "Bless You, O Lord, for the bounty of our table, the varied fruits we can be thankful for on this Thanksgiving Day of a troubled year"— his voice, so infrequently heard, croaked with the hollow imperfections of an old organ in an abandoned church—"Amen."

Then, as chairs were adjusted and napkins rustled, the necessary pause I'd been listening for arrived. "Someone here is a thief." I spoke clearly and repeated the accusation in even more measured tones: "Odd Henderson is a thief. He stole Miss Sook's cameo."

Napkins gleamed in suspended, immobilized hands. Men coughed, the Conklin sisters gasped in quadruplet unison and little Perk McCloud, Jr., began to hiccup, as very young children will when startled.

My friend, in a voice teetering between reproach and anguish, said, "Buddy doesn't mean that. He's only teasing."

"I do mean it. If you don't believe me, go look in your box. The cameo isn't there. Odd Henderson has it in his pocket."

54

"Buddy's had a bad croup," she murmured. "Don't blame him, Odd. He hasn't a notion what he's saying."

I said, "Go look in your box. I saw him take it."

Uncle B., staring at me with an alarming wintriness, took charge. "Maybe you'd better," he told Miss Sook. "That should settle the matter."

It was not often that my friend disobeyed her brother; she did not now. But her pallor, the mortified angle of her shoulders, revealed with what distaste she accepted the errand. She was gone only a minute, but her absence seemed an eon. Hostility sprouted and surged around the table like a thorn-encrusted vine growing with uncanny speed—and the victim trapped in its tendrils was not the accused, but his accuser. Stomach sickness gripped me; Odd, on the other hand, seemed calm as a corpse.

Miss Sook returned, smiling. "Shame on you, Buddy," she chided, shaking a finger. "Playing that kind of joke. My cameo was exactly where I left it."

Uncle B. said, "Buddy, I want to hear you apologize to our guest."

"No, he don't have to do that," Odd Henderson said, rising. "He was telling the truth." He dug into his pocket and put the cameo on the table. "I wish I had some excuse to give. But I ain't got none." Starting for the door, he said, "You must be a special lady, Miss Sook, to fib for me like that." And then, damn his soul, he walked right out of there.

So did I. Except I ran. I pushed back my chair, knocking it over. The crash triggered Queenie; she scooted from under the table, barked and bared her teeth. And Miss Sook, as I went past her, tried to stop me: "Buddy!" But I wanted no part of her *or* Queenie. That dog had snarled at me and my friend had taken Odd Henderson's side, she'd lied to save his skin, betrayed our friendship, my love: things I'd thought could never happen.

Simpson's pasture lay below the house, a meadow brilliant with high November gold and russet grass. At the edge of the pasture there were a gray barn, a pig corral, a fenced-in chicken yard and a smokehouse. It was the smokehouse I slipped into, a black chamber cool on even the hottest summer days. It had a dirt floor and a smoke pit that smelled of hickory cinders and creosote; rows of hams hung from rafters. It was a place I'd always been wary of, but now its darkness seemed sheltering. I fell on the ground, my ribs heaving like the gills of a beach-stranded fish; and I didn't care that I was demolishing my one nice suit, the one with long trousers, by thrashing about on the floor in a messy mixture of earth and ashes and pork grease.

One thing I knew: I was going to quit that house, that town, that night. Hit the road. Hop a freight and head for California. Make my living shining shoes in Hollywood. Fred Astaire's shoes. Clark Gable's. Or—maybe I just might become a movie star myself. Look at Jackie Cooper. Oh, they'd be sorry then. When I was rich and famous and refused to answer their letters and even telegrams, probably.

Suddenly I thought of something that would make them even sorrier. The door to the shed was ajar, and a knife of sunshine exposed a shelf supporting several bottles. Dusty bottles with skull-and-crossbone labels. If I drank from one of those, then all of them up there in the dining room, the whole swilling and gobbling caboodle, would know what sorry was. It was worth it, if only to witness Uncle B.'s remorse when they found me cold and stiff on the smokehouse floor; worth it to hear the human wails and Queenie's howls as my coffin was lowered into cemetery depths.

The only hitch was, I wouldn't actually be able to see or hear any of this: how could I, being dead? And unless one can observe the guilt and regret of the mourners, surely there is nothing satisfactory about being dead?

Uncle B. must have forbidden Miss Sook to go look for me until the last guest had left the table. It was late afternoon before I heard her voice floating across the pasture; she called my name softly, forlornly as a mourning dove. I stayed where I was and did not answer.

It was Queenie who found me; she came sniffing around the smokehouse and yapped when she caught my scent, then entered and crawled toward me and licked my hand, an ear and a cheek; she knew she had treated me badly.

Presently, the door swung open and the light widened. My friend said, "Come here, Buddy." And I wanted to go to her. When she saw me, she laughed. "Goodness, boy. You look dipped in tar and all ready for feathering." But there were no recriminations or references to my ruined suit.

Queenie trotted off to pester some cows; and trailing after her into the pasture, we sat down on a tree stump.

"I saved you a drumstick," she said, handing me a parcel wrapped in waxed paper. "And your favorite piece of turkey. The pulley."

The hunger that direr sensations had numbed now hit me like a belly-punch. I gnawed the drumstick clean, then stripped the pulley, the sweet part of the turkey around the wishbone.

While I was eating, Miss Sook put her arm around my shoulders. "There's just this I want to say, Buddy. Two wrongs never made a right. It was wrong of him to take the cameo. But we don't know why he took it. Maybe he never meant to keep it. Whatever his reason, it can't have been calculated. Which is why what you did was much worse: you *planned* to humiliate him. It was deliberate. Now listen to me, Buddy: there is only one unpardonable sin—*deliberate cruelty*. All else can be forgiven. That, never. Do you understand me, Buddy?"

I did, dimly, and time has taught me that she was right.

But at that moment I mainly comprehended that because my revenge had failed, my method must have been wrong. Odd Henderson had emerged—how? why?—as someone superior to me, even more honest.

"Do you, Buddy? Understand?"

"Sort of. Pull," I said, offering her one prong of the wishbone.

We split it; my half was the larger, which entitled me to a wish. She wanted to know what I'd wished.

"That you're still my friend."

"Dumbhead," she said, and hugged me.

"Forever?"

"I won't be here forever, Buddy. Nor will you." Her voice sank like the sun on the pasture's horizon, was silent a second and then climbed with the strength of a new sun. "But yes, forever. The Lord willing, you'll be here long after I've gone. And as long as you remember me, then we'll always be together." . . .

Afterward, Odd Henderson let me alone. He started tussling with a boy his own age, Squirrel McMillan. And the next year, because of Odd's poor grades and general bad conduct, our school principal wouldn't allow him to attend classes, so he spent the winter working as a hand on a dairy farm. The last time I saw him was shortly before he hitchhiked to Mobile, joined the Merchant Marine and disappeared. It must have been the year before I was packed off to a miserable fate in a military academy, and two years prior to my friend's death. That would make it the autumn of 1934.

Miss Sook had summoned me to the garden; she had transplanted a blossoming chrysanthemum bush into a tin washtub and needed help to haul it up the steps onto the front porch, where it would make a fine display. It was heavier than forty fat pirates, and while we were struggling with it ineffectually, Odd Henderson passed along the road. He paused at the garden gate and then opened it, saying, "Let me do that for you, ma'am." Life on a dairy farm had done him a lot of good; he'd thickened, his arms were sinewy and his red coloring had deepened to a ruddy brown. Airily he lifted the big tub and placed it on the porch.

My friend said, "I'm obliged to you, sir. That was neighborly."

"Nothing," he said, still ignoring me.

Miss Sook snapped the stems of her showiest blooms. "Take these to your mother," she told him, handing him the bouquet. "And give her my love."

"Thank you, ma'am. I will."

"Oh, Odd," she called, after he'd regained the road, "be careful! They're lions, you know." But he was already out of hearing. We watched until he turned a bend at the corner, innocent of the menace he carried, the chrysanthemums that burned, that growled and roared against a greenly lowering dusk.

A CHRISTMAS MEMORY

for Catherine Wood

Imagine a morning in late November. A coming of winter morning more than twenty years ago. Consider the kitchen of a spreading old house in a country town. A great black stove is its main feature; but there is also a big round table and a fireplace with two rocking chairs placed in front of it. Just today the fireplace commenced its seasonal roar.

A woman with shorn white hair is standing at the kitchen window. She is wearing tennis shoes and a shapeless gray sweater over a summery calico dress. She is small and sprightly, like a bantam hen; but, due to a long youthful illness, her shoulders are pitifully hunched. Her face is remarkable—not unlike Lincoln's, craggy like that, and tinted by sun and wind; but it is delicate too, finely boned, and her eyes are sherry-colored and timid. "Oh my," she exclaims, her breath smoking the windowpane, "it's fruitcake weather!"

The person to whom she is speaking is myself. I am seven; she is sixty-something. We are cousins, very distant ones, and we have lived together—well, as long as I can remember. Other people inhabit the house, relatives; and though they have power over us, and frequently make us cry, we are not, on the whole, too much aware of them. We are each other's best friend. She calls me Buddy, in memory of a boy who was formerly her best friend. The other Buddy died in the 1880's, when she was still a child. She is still a child.

"I knew it before I got out of bed," she says, turning away from the window with a purposeful excitement in her eyes. "The courthouse bell sounded so cold and clear. And there were no birds singing; they've gone to warmer country, yes indeed. Oh, Buddy, stop stuffing biscuit and fetch our buggy. Help me find my hat. We've thirty cakes to bake."

It's always the same: a morning arrives in November, and my friend, as though officially inaugurating the Christmas time of year that exhilarates her imagination and fuels the blaze of her heart, announces: "It's fruitcake weather! Fetch our buggy. Help me find my hat."

The hat is found, a straw cartwheel corsaged with velvet roses out-of-doors has faded: it once belonged to a more fashionable relative. Together, we guide our buggy, a dilapidated baby carriage, out to the garden and into a grove of pecan trees. The buggy is mine; that is, it was bought for me when I was born. It is made of wicker, rather unraveled, and the wheels wobble like a drunkard's legs. But it is a faithful object; springtimes, we take it to the woods and fill it with flowers, herbs, wild fern for our porch pots; in the summer, we pile it with picnic paraphernalia and sugar-cane fishing poles and roll it down to the edge of a creek; it has its winter uses, too: as a truck for hauling firewood from the yard to the kitchen, as a warm bed for Queenie, our tough little orange and white rat terrier who has survived distemper and two rattlesnake bites. Queenie is trotting beside it now.

Three hours later we are back in the kitchen hulling a heaping buggyload of windfall pecans. Our backs hurt from gathering them: how hard they were to find (the main crop having been shaken off the trees and sold by the orchard's owners, who are not us) among the concealing leaves, the frosted, deceiving grass. Caarackle! A cheery crunch, scraps of miniature thunder sound as the shells collapse and the golden mound of sweet oily ivory meat mounts in the milk-glass bowl. Queenie begs to taste, and now and again my friend sneaks her a mite, though insisting we deprive ourselves. "We mustn't, Buddy. If we start, we won't stop. And there's scarcely enough as there is. For thirty cakes." The kitchen is growing dark. Dusk turns the window into a mirror: our reflections mingle with the rising moon as we work by the fireside in the firelight. At last, when the moon is quite high, we toss the final hull into the fire and, with joined sighs, watch it catch flame. The buggy is empty, the bowl is brimful.

We eat our supper (cold biscuits, bacon, blackberry jam) and discuss tomorrow. Tomorrow the kind of work I like best begins: buying. Cherries and citron, ginger and vanilla and canned Hawaiian pineapple, rinds and raisins and walnuts and whiskey and oh, so much flour, butter, so many eggs, spices, flavorings: why, we'll need a pony to pull the buggy home.

But before these purchases can be made, there is the

question of money. Neither of us has any. Except for skinflint sums persons in the house occasionally provide (a dime is considered very big money); or what we earn ourselves from various activities: holding rummage sales, selling buckets of hand-picked blackberries, jars of home-made jam and apple jelly and peach preserves, rounding up flowers for funerals and weddings. Once we won seventy-ninth prize, five dollars, in a national football contest. Not that we know a fool thing about football. It's just that we enter any contest we hear about: at the moment our hopes are centered on the fifty-thousand-dollar Grand Prize being offered to name a new brand of coffee (we suggested "A.M."; and, after some hesitation, for my friend thought it perhaps sacrilegious, the slogan "A.M.! Amen!"). To tell the truth, our only *really* profitable enterprise was the Fun and Freak Museum we conducted in a back-yard woodshed two summers ago. The Fun was a stereopticon with slide views of Washington and New York lent us by a relative who had been to those places (she was furious when she discovered why we'd borrowed it); the Freak was a three-legged biddy chicken hatched by one of our own hens. Everybody hereabouts wanted to see that biddy: we charged grownups a nickel, kids two cents. And took in a good twenty dollars before the museum shut down due to the decease of the main attraction.

But one way and another we do each year accumulate Christmas savings, a Fruitcake Fund. These moneys we keep hidden in an ancient bead purse under a loose board under the floor under a chamber pot under my friend's bed. The purse is seldom removed from this safe location except to make a deposit, or, as happens every Saturday, a withdrawal; for on Saturdays I am allowed ten cents to go to the picture show. My friend has never been to a picture show, nor does she intend to: "I'd rather hear you tell the story, Buddy. That way I can imagine it more. Besides, a person my age shouldn't squander their eyes. When the Lord comes, let me see Him clear." In addition to never having seen a movie, she has never: eaten in a restaurant, traveled more than five miles from home, received or sent a telegram, read anything except funny papers and the Bible, worn cosmetics, cursed, wished someone harm, told a lie on purpose, let a hungry dog go hungry. Here are a few things she has done, does do: killed with a hoe the biggest rattlesnake ever seen in this county (sixteen rattles), dip snuff (secretly), tame hummingbirds (just try it) till they balance on her finger, tell ghost stories (we both believe in ghosts) so tingling they chill you in July, talk to herself, take walks in the rain, grow the prettiest japonicas in town, know the recipe for every sort of old-time Indian cure, including a magical wart-remover.

Now, with supper finished, we retire to the room in a faraway part of the house where my friend sleeps in a scrap-quilt-covered iron bed painted rose pink, her favorite color. Silently, wallowing in the pleasures of conspiracy, we take the bead purse from its secret place and spill its contents on the scrap quilt. Dollar bills, tightly rolled and green as May buds. Somber fifty-cent pieces, heavy enough to weight a dead man's eyes. Lovely dimes, the liveliest coin, the one that really jingles. Nickels and quarters, worn smooth as creek pebbles. But mostly a hateful heap of bitter-odored pennies. Last summer others in the house contracted to pay us a penny for every twenty-five flies we killed. Oh, the carnage of August: the flies that flew to heaven! Yet it was not work in which we took pride. And, as we sit counting pennies, it is as though we were back tabulating dead flies. Neither of us has a head for figures; we count slowly, lose track, start again. According to her calculations, we have $12.73. According to mine, exactly $13. "I do hope you're wrong, Buddy. We can't mess around with thirteen. The cakes will fall. Or put somebody in the cemetery. Why, I wouldn't dream of getting out of bed on the thirteenth." This is true: she always spends thirteenths in bed. So, to be on the safe side, we subtract a penny and toss it out the window.

Of the ingredients that go into our fruitcakes, whiskey is the most expensive, as well as the hardest to obtain: State laws forbid its sale. But everybody knows you can buy a bottle from Mr. Haha Jones. And the next day, having completed our more prosaic shopping, we set out for Mr. Haha's business address, a "sinful" (to quote public opinion) fish-fry and dancing café down by the river. We've been there before, and on the same errand; but in previous years our dealings have been with Haha's wife, an iodine-dark Indian woman with brassy peroxided hair and a dead-tired disposition. Actually, we've never laid eyes on her husband, though we've heard that he's an Indian too. A giant with razor scars across his cheeks.

A Christmas Memory

They call him Haha because he's so gloomy, a man who never laughs. As we approach his café (a large log cabin festooned inside and out with chains of garish-gay naked light bulbs and standing by the river's muddy edge under the shade of river trees where moss drifts through the branches like gray mist) our steps slow down. Even Queenie stops prancing and sticks close by. People have been murdered in Haha's café. Cut to pieces. Hit on the head. There's a case coming up in court next month. Naturally these goings-on happen at night when the colored lights cast crazy patterns and the victrola wails. In the daytime Haha's is shabby and deserted. I knock at the door, Queenie barks, my friend calls: "Mrs. Haha, ma'am? Anyone to home?"

Footsteps. The door opens. Our hearts overturn. It's

Mr. Haha Jones himself! And he *is* a giant; he *does* have scars; he *doesn't* smile. No, he glowers at us through Satan-tilted eyes and demands to know: "What you want with Haha?"

For a moment we are too paralyzed to tell. Presently my friend half-finds her voice, a whispery voice at best: "If you please, Mr. Haha, we'd like a quart of your finest whiskey."

His eyes tilt more. Would you believe it? Haha is smiling! Laughing, too. "Which one of you is a drinkin' man?"

"It's for making fruitcakes, Mr. Haha. Cooking."

This sobers him. He frowns. "That's no way to waste good whiskey." Nevertheless, he retreats into the shadowed café and seconds later appears carrying a bottle of daisy-yellow unlabeled liquor. He demonstrates its sparkle in the sunlight and says: "Two dollars."

We pay him with nickels and dimes and pennies. Suddenly, as he jangles the coins in his hand like a fistful of dice, his face softens. "Tell you what," he proposes, pouring the money back into our bead purse, "just send me one of them fruitcakes instead."

"Well," my friend remarks on our way home, "there's a lovely man. We'll put an extra cup of raisins in *his* cake."

The black stove, stoked with coal and firewood, glows like a lighted pumpkin. Eggbeaters whirl, spoons spin round in bowls of butter and sugar, vanilla sweetens the air, ginger spices it; melting, nose-tingling odors saturate the kitchen, suffuse the house, drift out to the world on puffs of chimney smoke. In four days our work is done. Thirty-one cakes, dampened with whiskey, bask on window sills and shelves.

Who are they for?

Friends. Not necessarily neighbor friends: indeed, the larger share is intended for persons we've met maybe once, perhaps not at all. People who've struck our fancy. Like President Roosevelt. Like the Reverend and Mrs. J. C. Lucey, Baptist missionaries to Borneo who lectured here last winter. Or the little knife grinder who comes through town twice a year. Or Abner Packer, the driver of the six o'clock bus from Mobile, who exchanges waves with us every day as he passes in a dust-cloud whoosh. Or the young Wistons, a California couple whose car one afternoon broke down outside the house and who spent a pleasant hour chatting with us on the porch (young Mr. Wiston snapped our picture, the only one we've ever had taken). Is it because my friend is shy with everyone *except* strangers that these strangers, and merest acquaintances, seem to us our truest friends? I think yes. Also, the scrapbooks we keep of thank-you's on White House stationery, time-to-time communications from California and Borneo, the knife grinder's penny post cards, make us feel connected to eventful worlds beyond the kitchen with its view of a sky that stops.

Now a nude December fig branch grates against the window. The kitchen is empty, the cakes are gone; yesterday we carted the last of them to the post office, where the cost of stamps turned our purse inside out. We're broke. That rather depresses me, but my friend insists on celebrating—with two inches of whiskey left in Haha's bottle. Queenie has a spoonful in a bowl of coffee (she likes her coffee chicory-flavored and strong). The rest we divide between a pair of jelly glasses. We're both quite awed at the prospect of drinking straight whiskey; the taste of it brings screwed-up expressions and sour shudders. But by and by we begin to sing, the two of us singing different songs simultaneously. I don't know the words to mine, just: *Come on along, come on along, to the dark-town strutters' ball.* But I can dance: that's what I mean to be, a tap-dancer in the movies. My dancing shadow rollicks on the walls; our voices rock the chinaware; we giggle: as if unseen hands were tickling us. Queenie rolls on her back, her paws plow the air, something like a grin stretches her black lips. Inside myself, I feel warm and sparky as those crumbling logs, carefree as the wind in the chimney. My friend waltzes round the stove, the hem of her poor calico skirt pinched between her fingers as though it were a party dress: *Show me the way to go home*, she sings, her tennis shoes squeaking on the floor. *Show me the way to go home.*

Enter: two relatives. Very angry. Potent with eyes that scold, tongues that scald. Listen to what they have to say, the words tumbling together into a wrathful tune: "A child of seven! whiskey on his breath! are you out of your mind? feeding a child of seven! must be loony! road to ruination! remember Cousin Kate? Uncle Charlie? Uncle Charlie's brother-in-law? shame! scandal! humiliation! kneel, pray, beg the Lord!"

Queenie sneaks under the stove. My friend gazes at her

shoes, her chin quivers, she lifts her skirt and blows her nose and runs to her room. Long after the town has gone to sleep and the house is silent except for the chimings of clocks and the sputter of fading fires, she is weeping into a pillow already as wet as a widow's handkerchief.

"Don't cry," I say, sitting at the bottom of her bed and shivering despite my flannel nightgown that smells of last winter's cough syrup, "don't cry," I beg, teasing her toes, tickling her feet, "you're too old for that."

"It's because," she hiccups, "I *am* too old. Old and funny."

"Not funny. Fun. More fun than anybody. Listen. If you don't stop crying you'll be so tired tomorrow we can't go cut a tree."

She straightens up. Queenie jumps on the bed (where

Queenie is not allowed) to lick her cheeks. "I know where we'll find real pretty trees, Buddy. And holly, too. With berries big as your eyes. It's way off in the woods. Farther than we've ever been. Papa used to bring us Christmas trees from there: carry them on his shoulder. That's fifty years ago. Well, now: I can't wait for morning."

Morning. Frozen rime lusters the grass; the sun, round as an orange and orange as hot-weather moons, balances on the horizon, burnishes the silvered winter woods. A wild turkey calls. A renegade hog grunts in the undergrowth. Soon, by the edge of knee-deep, rapid-running water, we have to abandon the buggy. Queenie wades the stream first, paddles across barking complaints at the swiftness of the current, the pneumonia-making coldness of it. We follow, holding our shoes and equipment (a hatchet, a burlap sack) above our heads. A mile more: of chastising thorns, burs and briers that catch at our clothes; of rusty pine needles brilliant with gaudy fungus and molted feathers. Here, there, a flash, a flutter, an ecstasy of shrillings remind us that not all the birds have flown south. Always, the path unwinds through lemony sun pools and pitch-black vine tunnels. Another creek to cross: a disturbed armada of speckled trout froths the water round us, and frogs the size of plates practice belly flops; beaver workmen are building a dam. On the farther shore, Queenie shakes herself and trembles. My friend shivers, too: not with cold but enthusiasm. One of her hat's ragged roses sheds a petal as she lifts her head and inhales the pine-heavy air. "We're almost there; can you smell it, Buddy?" she says, as though we were approaching an ocean.

And, indeed, it is a kind of ocean. Scented acres of holiday trees, prickly-leafed holly. Red berries shiny as Chinese bells: black crows swoop upon them screaming. Having stuffed our burlap sacks with enough greenery and crimson to garland a dozen windows, we set about choosing a tree. "It should be," muses my friend, "twice as tall as a boy. So a boy can't steal the star." The one we pick is twice as tall as me. A brave handsome brute that survives thirty hatchet strokes before it keels with a creaking rending cry. Lugging it like a kill, we commence the long trek out. Every few yards we abandon the struggle, sit down and pant. But we have the strength of triumphant huntsmen; that and the tree's virile, icy perfume revive us, goad us on. Many compliments accompany our sunset return along the red clay road to town;

but my friend is sly and noncommittal when passers-by praise the treasure perched in our buggy: what a fine tree and where did it come from? "Yonderways," she murmurs vaguely. Once a car stops and the rich mill owner's lazy wife leans out and whines: "Giveya two-bits cash for that ol tree." Ordinarily my friend is afraid of saying no; but on this occasion she promptly shakes her head: "We wouldn't take a dollar." The mill owner's wife persists. "A dollar, my foot! Fifty cents. That's my last offer. Goodness, woman, you can get another one." In answer, my friend gently reflects: "I doubt it. There's never two of anything."

Home: Queenie slumps by the fire and sleeps till to-morrow, snoring loud as a human.

A trunk in the attic contains: a shoebox of ermine tails (off the opera cape of a curious lady who once rented a room in the house), coils of frazzled tinsel gone gold with age, one silver star, a brief rope of dilapidated, undoubtedly dangerous candy-like light bulbs. Excellent decorations, as far as they go, which isn't far enough: my friend wants our tree to blaze "like a Baptist window," droop with weighty snows of ornament. But we can't afford the made-in-Japan splendors at the five-and-dime. So we do what we've always done: sit for days at the kitchen table with scissors and crayons and stacks of colored paper. I make sketches and my friend cuts them out: lots of cats, fish too (because they're easy to draw), some apples, some watermelons, a few winged angels devised from saved-up sheets of Hershey-bar tin foil. We use safety pins to attach these creations to the tree; as a final touch, we sprinkle the branches with shredded cotton (picked in August for this purpose). My friend, surveying the effect, clasps her hands together. "Now honest, Buddy. Doesn't it look good enough to eat?" Queenie tries to eat an angel.

After weaving and ribboning holly wreaths for all the front windows, our next project is the fashioning of family gifts. Tie-dye scarves for the ladies, for the men a home-brewed lemon and licorice and aspirin syrup to be taken "at the first Symptoms of a Cold and after Hunting." But when it comes time for making each other's gift, my friend and I separate to work secretly. I would like to buy her a pearl-handled knife, a radio, a whole pound of chocolate-covered cherries (we tasted some once, and she always swears: "I could live on them, Buddy, Lord yes I could—and that's not taking His name in vain"). Instead, I am building her a kite. She would like to give me a bicycle (she's said so on several million occasions: "If only I could, Buddy. It's bad enough in life to do without something *you* want; but confound it, what gets my goat is not being able to give somebody something you want *them* to have. Only one of these days I will, Buddy. Locate you a bike. Don't ask how. Steal it, maybe"). Instead, I'm fairly certain that she is building me a kite— the same as last year, and the year before: the year before that we exchanged slingshots. All of which is fine by me. For we are champion kite-fliers who study the wind like sailors; my friend, more accomplished than I, can get a kite aloft when there isn't enough breeze to carry clouds.

Christmas Eve afternoon we scrape together a nickel and go to the butcher's to buy Queenie's traditional gift, a good gnawable beef bone. The bone, wrapped in funny paper, is placed high in the tree near the silver star. Queenie knows it's there. She squats at the foot of the tree staring up in a trance of greed: when bedtime arrives she refuses to budge. Her excitement is equaled by my own. I kick the covers and turn my pillow as though it were a scorching summer's night. Somewhere a rooster crows: falsely, for the sun is still on the other side of the world.

"Buddy, are you awake?" It is my friend, calling from her room, which is next to mine; and an instant later she is sitting on my bed holding a candle. "Well, I can't sleep a hoot," she declares. "My mind's jumping like a jack rabbit. Buddy, do you think Mrs. Roosevelt will serve our cake at dinner?" We huddle in the bed, and she squeezes my hand I-love-you. "Seems like your hand used to be so much smaller. I guess I hate to see you grow up. When you're grown up, will we still be friends?" I say always. "But I feel so bad, Buddy. I wanted so bad to give you a bike. I tried to sell my cameo Papa gave me. Buddy"—she hesitates, as though embarrassed—"I made you another kite." Then I confess that I made her one, too; and we laugh. The candle burns too short to hold. Out it goes, exposing the starlight, the stars spinning at the window like a visible caroling that slowly, slowly daybreak silences. Possibly we doze; but the beginnings of dawn splash us like cold water: we're up, wide-eyed and wandering while we wait for others to waken. Quite deliberately my friend drops a kettle on the kitchen floor. I tap-dance in front of closed doors. One by one the household emerges, looking as though they'd like to kill us both; but it's Christmas, so they can't. First, a gorgeous breakfast: just everything you can imagine— from flapjacks and fried squirrel to hominy grits and honey-in-the-comb. Which puts everyone in a good humor except my friend and me. Frankly, we're so impatient to get at the presents we can't eat a mouthful.

Well, I'm disappointed. Who wouldn't be? With socks, a Sunday school shirt, some handkerchiefs, a hand-me-down sweater and a year's subscription to a religious magazine for children. *The Little Shepherd.* It makes me boil. It really does.

My friend has a better haul. A sack of Satsumas, that's

her best present. She is proudest, however, of a white wool shawl knitted by her married sister. But she *says* her favorite gift is the kite I built her. And it *is* very beautiful; though not as beautiful as the one she made me, which is blue and scattered with gold and green Good Conduct stars; moreover, my name is painted on it, "Buddy."

"Buddy, the wind is blowing."

The wind is blowing, and nothing will do till we've run to a pasture below the house where Queenie has scooted to bury her bone (and where, a winter hence, Queenie will be buried, too). There, plunging through the healthy waist-high grass, we unreel our kites, feel them twitching at the string like sky fish as they swim into the wind. Satisfied, sun-warmed, we sprawl in the grass and peel Satsumas and watch our kites cavort. Soon I forget the socks and hand-me-down sweater. I'm as happy as if we'd already won the fifty-thousand-dollar Grand Prize in that coffee-naming contest.

"My, how foolish I am!" my friend cries, suddenly alert, like a woman remembering too late she has biscuits in the oven. "You know what I've always thought?" she asks in a tone of discovery, and not smiling at me but a point beyond. "I've always thought a body would have to be sick and dying before they saw the Lord. And I imagined that when He came it would be like looking at the Baptist window: pretty as colored glass with the sun pouring through, such a shine you don't know it's getting dark. And it's been a comfort: to think of that shine taking away all the spooky feeling. But I'll wager it never happens. I'll wager at the very end a body realizes the

Lord has already shown Himself. That things as they are"—her hand circles in a gesture that gathers clouds and kites and grass and Queenie pawing earth over her bone—"just what they've always seen, was seeing Him. As for me, I could leave the world with today in my eyes."

This is our last Christmas together.

Life separates us. Those who Know Best decide that I belong in a military school. And so follows a miserable succession of bugle-blowing prisons, grim reveille-ridden summer camps. I have a new home too. But it doesn't count. Home is where my friend is, and there I never go.

And there she remains, puttering around the kitchen. Alone with Queenie. Then alone. ("Buddy dear," she writes in her wild hard-to-read script, "yesterday Jim Macy's horse kicked Queenie bad. Be thankful she didn't feel much. I wrapped her in a Fine Linen sheet and rode her in the buggy down to Simpson's pasture where she can be with all her Bones . . ."). For a few Novembers she continues to bake her fruitcakes single-handed; not as many, but some: and, of course, she always sends me "the best of the batch." Also, in every letter she encloses a dime wadded in toilet paper: "See a picture show and write me the story." But gradually in her letters she tends to confuse me with her other friend, the Buddy who died in the 1880's; more and more thirteenths are not the only days she stays in bed: a morning arrives in November, a leafless birdless coming of winter morning, when she cannot rouse herself to exclaim: "Oh my, it's fruitcake weather!"

And when that happens, I know it. A message saying so merely confirms a piece of news some secret vein had already received, severing from me an irreplaceable part of myself, letting it loose like a kite on a broken string. That is why, walking across a school campus on this particular December morning, I keep searching the sky. As if I expected to see, rather like hearts, a lost pair of kites hurrying toward heaven.

ABOUT THE AUTHOR

Until he was ten years old, Truman Capote lived with a family of distant and elderly cousins in a small town in rural Alabama. Both *A Christmas Memory* and *The Thanksgiving Visitor* are frankly autobiographical stories about those years, and especially of his relationship with one of the cousins, Miss Sook Faulk. The photograph on the cover of this boxed edition is of the author and Miss Faulk, who died in 1938 while Mr. Capote was a student at a military academy in New York State.